# You Must Be Sleepy

Written By:

## HEATHER ANN LYNN

From the author, it is my deepest gratitude to be able to write a book about the situations nice and kind in my children's collection series. The books written and published are examples of exlempry behavior in families, and the joy a team makes in their unit together.

With that being said, I dedicate this to my two loving boys, Bradley and Vincent. I hope that "You Must Be Sleepy" will bring great memories now and later in our many fun routine life living situations.

Mom and Brother build battleships
with Batmen, swords, and capes.

# While Vincent plays along everything is great!

And as our stream of kids bopping songs play,
the music is warm and bright,

The boys soon pick-up their swords
and start a battle fight!

Come and get me!

6

Here I am!

The battle starts the night.

9

Later on, Mom chimes in, "Boys, you fought with all your might, now all swords to the floor! Come on! It's a weeknight!"

The boys make-out to the table,

And diving for
their plates,

conversation filled
the air then Mom
looked so joyful
and proud.

15

And as we've finished for the evening,
It is blissful and loud, Please
and Thank-you's are
shouted out.

17

"It's time, It's time!" Mom clapped her hands, "All dishes to the sink!"

The Boys tired and groggy picked up their speed through bath and brushing teeth.

Next things pajamas and book, and tuck in all tight.

"Mom loves you much, Now
snuggle in, Goodnight!"

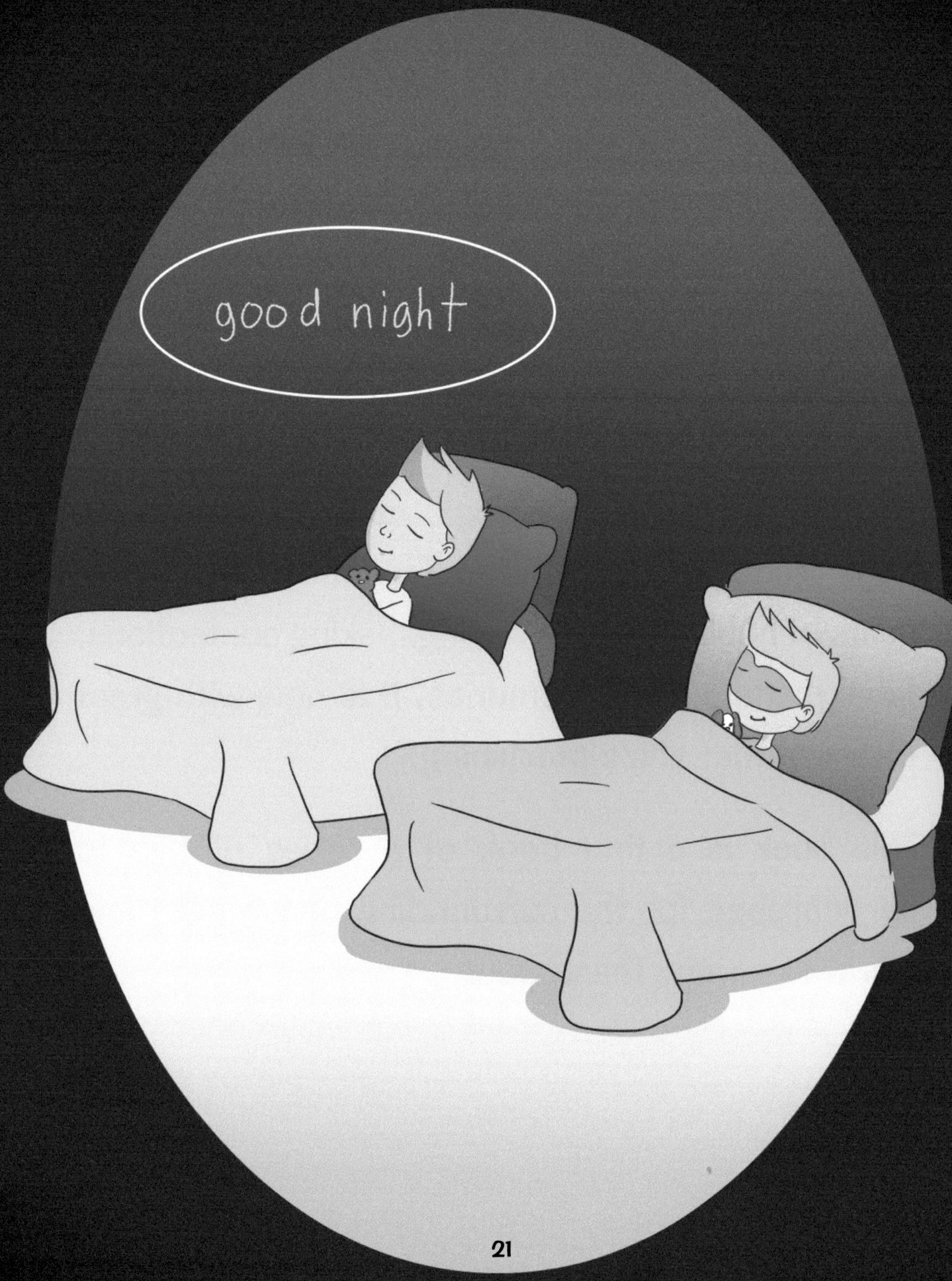
good night

## About the author

Heather Ann Lynn is a single mom of two young boys living in the suburbs Frederick, MD. After years of hobby creative writing, baking confections, family, and making memories, it is now with great pleasure that she's publishing.

This book is a first book of a series of five to be published for the surrounding community and world to enjoy. Thank you!

ISBN:   Softcover        978-1-5434-6707-9
        Hardcover        978-1-5434-6706-2
        EBook            978-1-5434-6708-6

Print information available on the last page

Rev. date: 09/12/2018

To order additional copies of this book, contact:
Xlibris
1-888-795-4274
www.Xlibris.com
Orders@Xlibris.com

Printed in the United States
By Bookmasters